A Note to Parents and Caregivers:

Read-it! Joke Books are for children who are moving ahead on the amazing road to reading. These fun books support the acquisition and extension of reading skills as well as a love of books.

Published by the same company that produces *Read-it!* Readers, these books introduce the question/answer pattern that helps children expand their thinking about language structure and book formats.

When sharing a book with your child, read in short stretches, pausing often to talk about the pictures and the meaning of the book. The question/answer format works well for this purpose and provides an opportunity to talk about the language and meaning of the jokes. Have your child turn the pages and point to the pictures and familiar words. Read the story in a natural voice; have fun creating the voices of characters or emphasizing some important words. And be sure to reread favorite parts.

There is no right or wrong way to share books with children. Find time to read with your child, and pass on the legacy of literacy.

Adria F. Klein, Ph.D.
Professor Emeritus
California State University
San Bernardino, California

Managing Editor: Bob Temple

Creative Director: Terri Foley

Editor: Sara E. Hoffmann

Designers: John Moldstad, Amy Bailey

Page production: Picture Window Books

The illustrations in this book were prepared digitally.

Picture Window Books

5115 Excelsior Boulevard

Suite 232

Minneapolis, MN 55416

1-877-845-8392

www.picturewindowbooks.com

Printed in the United States of America.

Library of Congress Cataloging-in-Publication Data

Dahl, Michael.

School daze : a book of riddles about school / written by Michael Dahl ;
illustrated by Garry Nichols.

p. cm.—(Read-it! joke books)

ISBN 1-4048-0231-2

1. Riddles, Juvenile. 2. Schools—Juvenile humor.

3. Education—Juvenile humor. I. Nichols, Garry. ill. II. Title.

PN6371.5 .D35 2003

818'.602—dc21

2003004585

School
Daze

A Book of Riddles About School

Michael Dahl • Illustrated by Garry Nichols

Reading Advisers:
Adria F. Klein, Ph.D.
Professor Emeritus, California State University
San Bernardino, California

Susan Kesselring, M.A., Literacy Educator
Rosemount-Apple Valley-Eagan (Minnesota) School District

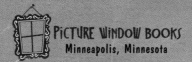
PiCTURE WiNDOW BOOKS
Minneapolis, Minnesota

Who takes little monsters to school?

Their mummies.

5

Why was the broom late for school?

It overswept.

What's the difference between a school bus driver and a cold?

One knows the stops,
and the other stops the nose.

Why did the balloon get good grades?

It always rose to the top of the class.

What does a teacher get if he puts all his students under a microscope?

A magnifying class.

Why was Cinderella thrown off the school's soccer team?

She ran away from the ball.

What do you call a student with a dictionary in his pocket?

Smarty pants.

What kind of band doesn't make music?

A rubber band. 13

What's the difference between a train and a teacher?

A train says, "Choo-choo," and a teacher says, "Spit out your gum!"

Why did the student bring a ladder to music class?

The teacher told him to sing higher. 15

In what school do you have to drop out to graduate?

Sky-diving school.

Why was the school clock punished?

It tocked too much during class.

Why do soccer players do well in school?

They really know
how to use
their heads. 19

Why is the basketball team so cool?

It has so many fans.

What did the teacher do with the cheese's homework?

She grated it.

What flies around
the school at night?

The alpha-bat.

What did the little turtles say to their teacher?

"You tortoise everything we know."